Disney PRINCESS

Beauty AND THE Beast

Belle and the Castle Puppy

Written by
Barbara Bazaldua

Illustrated by
Studio IBOIX, Marco Colletti,
and Elena Naggi

This book belongs to:

DISNEY PRINCESS

Beauty
AND
THE
Beast

Belle and the
Castle Puppy

DISNEY PRESS

Los Angeles • New York

Originally published by Disney Press © 2005 Disney Enterprises, Inc.

For information address Disney Press, 1200 Grand Central Avenue,
Glendale, California 91201.

ISBN 978-1-368-02798-4
FAC-023680-20154
Printed in Guangdong, China
First Box Set Edition, July 2018
3 5 7 9 10 8 6 4

For more Disney Press fun, visit www.disneybooks.com
This book was printed on paper created from a sustainable source.

$\mathcal{B}$*elle was strolling through* the castle garden one chilly spring day when she heard a whimpering sound. A puppy was huddled outside the castle gates. He looked cold and dirty.

"Oh, you poor thing!" Belle cried. "Let's get you warmed up and fed!"

She wrapped the puppy in her red cloak and hurried to the castle.

Belle and the enchanted objects gave the puppy a bath. The coatrack brought a towel.

When he was clean and dry, the puppy ate a bowl of warm stew.

"He's so cute! I hope we can keep him!" Chip the teacup exclaimed.

All the enchanted objects were happy to have a guest.
But the ottoman remembered when he had been a real
dog, just like the puppy. What if Belle and the Beast liked
this dog better? The ottoman tried to get Belle's attention.
With a funny little *grrr*, he raced around the kitchen. But
no one noticed.

A moment later, the puppy barked at the door.

"Do you want to go out to play?" Belle asked.

As Belle and the others followed the puppy outside,
they didn't see the ottoman slink out behind them and
walk in a different direction. They laughed as Belle threw
sticks for the puppy to fetch.

The Beast walked up to Belle a while later.

"Someone has dug up my roses!" he exclaimed.

Then the Beast saw the puppy. "Did that dog ruin my garden? Get rid of him—NOW!" the Beast roared as he stomped away.

A moment later, the ottoman ran past Belle and the others. His legs were muddy.

"The ottoman dug up the garden!" Belle exclaimed.

"But why?" asked Lumiere the candelabrum.

As Belle watched the ottoman chase after the Beast, she suddenly understood.

"Oh, poor little guy," she said. "He just wanted some attention, too!"

Suddenly, the puppy raced after the ottoman, barking playfully. They both disappeared among the trees.

"What if they don't catch up to the Beast? They'll get lost!" Belle exclaimed. "I have to bring them back safely."

"But it's getting dark," Mrs. Potts protested.

Belle looked at the long shadows creeping through the forest. Clutching her cloak tightly, she took a deep breath and started toward the trees.

"Wait!" Lumiere called to Belle. "I'll come and light your way."

"Thank you," Belle said as she picked up the candelabrum. "I'm glad you're coming."

"Me too. I think," Lumiere replied. But his flames flickered nervously.

Belle walked along a path. She had come this way before.

"Puppy! Ottoman!" she called.

She hoped that they had met up with the Beast. She was looking forward to returning to the castle.

A moment later, something rustled in the bushes.

"What is that?" Lumiere whispered.

"I hope it's just squirrels," Belle answered.

"They must be very big squirrels," Lumiere replied.

Belle picked up a large stick. Then she and Lumiere walked on, calling for the puppy and the ottoman.

Belle realized that the puppy and ottoman had gotten lost. She was determined to find them.

A short while later, Belle heard loud barking.

"I think we found them!" Lumiere exclaimed.

Belle followed the sound until she came into a clearing. The ottoman and puppy stood under an enormous tree. The puppy was growling and barking loudly.

"What's wrong?" Belle wondered aloud. Then she looked around and gasped. Two large wolves were sitting nearby.

"The puppy is protecting the ottoman!" Lumiere exclaimed.

"He's too small to stop those wolves for long," Belle said. "He needs help!"

Quickly, Belle put Lumiere on the ground and lit the stick she had been carrying. She ran toward the wolves, swinging it.

"Get away! Get away!" she shouted.

But the wolves didn't move.

Just then, the Beast showed up. The wolves ran away, yelping with fear.

"The puppy tried to save the ottoman!" Belle told the Beast.

"They are brave little fellows," the Beast answered.

Cradling the puppy in one arm and the ottoman in the other, he led Belle to the castle.

Later that night, everyone settled by the fireplace.
Belle watched the Beast stroke the ottoman and feed
biscuits to the puppy.

"May the puppy stay until I can find him a home?"
she asked.

The Beast cleared his throat. "His home is here—
with us," he answered gruffly.

Belle smiled. She was glad that the Beast had
come around.

The very next day, the Beast presented the puppy and the ottoman with shiny badges. From now on, they would be the official protectors of the house.

Yip! Yip! Woof! Woof! They couldn't have been more excited.